Ella's Games

For my daughter, Isobel.

D.B.

For Luke & Hayley

and all the games we've played.

With love,

P.K.

First published by Scholastic Ltd. 2002
Published in 2016 by Caboodle Books Ltd.
Text copyright © David Bedford 2016
Illustrations copyright © Peter Kavanagh 2016
This edition designed by Mandy Stanley
ISBN 978-0-9954885-1-9

Ella's Games

Written by David Bedford

Illustrations by Peter Kavanagh

Ella's brothers played in the honeysuckle tub.

'**Can I play too?**' asked Ella.

'Sorry,' said Joe. 'You can't climb.'
'You're much too small,' said Jim.
'And you'd be scared,' said Jack.

So Ella went away
to play on her own,
and she found...

a cat's whisker.

So she made up a game.

'What's that?' asked Jack
when Ella came back.

'I'll tell you...' said Ella.

'It's a **whisker** from a **rainbow cat!**
The cat miaowed, "I'm going to chase you, Ella!"
So I plucked out one of his whiskers,
and **frightened** him away!'

Ya !

Miaow !

'Can I play in the honeysuckle tub now?' asked Ella. 'I won't be scared - I can frighten cats!'

'You *still* can't play with us,' said Jim, 'because you're much *too* small.'

So Ella went away to play on her own again, and found...

I know!

a fluffy flower.

Ha!

So she made up a game.

Ella's brothers were having a bath
when Ella came back.

'What's that?' asked Jim.

'I'll tell you...' said Ella.

'It's an **elephant tickler!**
I found an elephant having a mud bath.
He trumpeted, "**Help me,** Ella, I'm stuck!"
So I tickled his nose until he sniffed and
snuffled and then **SNEEZED** his way out.'

ATCHOOO!

'Now can I play in the honeysuckle tub?' asked Ella.
'It doesn't matter if I'm small - I can save elephants!'

'You still can't play with us,' said Joe,
'because you can't climb.'

So Ella went away to play
on her own once more,
and found...

Hmm...

a pointy stone.

Aha !

So she made up a game.

Ella's brothers were getting ready for bed when Ella came back.

'What's that?' asked Joe.

'I'll tell you...'
said Ella.

'It's a **dragon's** wobbly tooth!
I climbed all the way up to the
dragon's head, and plucked it out.
He was so pleased, he took me
flying round and round the clouds.'

That night, Ella's brothers couldn't sleep.
'Ella,' asked Jack, 'will you play with
us tomorrow? You *won't* be
scared - you frightened a rainbow cat!'
'You're *not* too small,' said Jim. 'You saved
an elephant!'
'And you *can* climb,' said Joe. 'You even
climbed a dragon!'

'All right,' said Ella happily.

'What shall we play?' asked Jack, Jim and Joe.

'I'll tell you...' said Ella.

And the next day, Jack,
Jim and Joe made ready
to sail across the sea

HMS Honey-suckle

in the **fantastic** new

adventure of...

Ella's Games

About the author...

David Bedford is the author of over 80 best-selling books for children, published in 30 different languages. His popular author visits have taken him to schools and libraries all around the UK and to countries as far away as Spain, Jordan, China, Sudan, Qatar and Abu Dhabi.

www.davidbedford.co.uk

About the illustrator...

Peter has illustrated over 160 books for many popular authors. He works as a storyteller using visual ideas that expand and enhance the words of the author. He enjoys visiting schools to share his love of drawing and stories.